Anonymous

The Hannibal and St. Joseph Railroad Company

have received by grant from congress over 600,000 acres of the choicest

farming and wood lands, the greater portion of which is now in the

market, and the remainder will be offered from time to time

Anonymous

The Hannibal and St. Joseph Railroad Company
*have received by grant from congress over 600,000 acres of the choicest farming
and wood lands, the greater portion of which is now in the market, and the
remainder will be offered from time to time*

ISBN/EAN: 9783337419301

Printed in Europe, USA, Canada, Australia, Japan

Cover: Foto ©Andreas Hilbeck / pixelio.de

More available books at **www.hansebooks.com**

600,000 ACRES

OF

HANNIBAL & ST. JOSEPH

RAILROAD LANDS,

IN

NORTH MISSOURI.

––––––•–•––––––

NOTICE TO PURCHASERS.

THE Lands offered for sale by the Hannibal and St. Joseph Railroad Company, were granted by the United States to the State of Missouri, by Act of Congress, approved June 10th, 1852.

By an additional act, approved August 3d, 1854, it was provided, that the Certificate of the Land Commissioner should vest the title in fee to the lands so certified, so far as embraced within the grant.

By an act, bearing date September 20th, 1852, the State of Missouri provided, "that all that portion of the lands granted to this State, by the act of Congress," above referred to, "so far as the same are applicable to the construction of a Railroad from the town of Hannibal to the town of St. Joseph, together

(3)

with all the rights and privileges thereto belonging, or in said act granted, shall vest in full and complete title in the Hannibal and St. Joseph Railroad Company."

The only conditions remaining to be considered, are contained in the fifth section of the act of Congress, making the grant, and are as follows:

" That the Lands hereby granted to said State, shall be disposed of by said State, only in manner following, that is to say:—That a quantity of land, not exceeding one hundred and twenty sections on each road, and included within a continuous length of twenty miles of said road, may be sold ; and when the Governor of said State shall certify to the Secretary of the Interior, that said twenty miles of said road is completed, then another like quantity of land, hereby granted, may be sold, and so from time to time, until said road is completed; and if said road be not completed within ten years, no further sale shall be made, and the land unsold shall revert to the United States."

The entire road being now completed and opened for use, the principal portion of these lands are offered for sale, and the remainder will be put in market from time to time, as the necessary examination and appraisal can be made.

By permission of the State, granted in the act of September 20th, 1852, all of these lands have been mortgaged to Trustees, to secure the payment of the Bonds of the Company, to the amount of $5,000,000.

As among the conditions of this mortgage, it is provided, that the Hannibal and St. Joseph Railroad Company, " shall be, at all times, at liberty to contract for the sale of any of the divisions or parcels of said land, and upon the payment of such purchase money to said parties of the second part, (the Trustees,) said parties of the second part, or any two of them, shall, by proper deeds or instruments by them executed, join in a release and conveyance of such parcel or parcels of land, to the purchasers thereof."

Such conveyance by the Trustees and the Company jointly, would constitute a perfect and indefeasible title to the land so conveyed.

When payment is made in full, the purchaser at once obtains his title. If the sale is on credit, the title is not given until final payment is made, but the purchaser receives a contract, stipulating that such title will be given on full payment and compliance with the conditions specified therein.

Payment for lands purchased, can be made in the Land Bonds of the Company, or in cash; and, if in the latter, it is applied to the purchase of such Bonds, and the particular tract is at once exempt from liability, and a perfect title given—being, in fact, the first conveyance under the authority of the General Government.

From this it appears, that while the Bondholders are secured, the rights of purchasers are also amply protected.

JOSIAH HUNT,
Land Commissioner H. & St. Jo. R. R.

DESCRIPTION OF ROAD

AND LOCATION OF LAND.

The Hannibal and St. Joseph Railroad commences at Hannibal, on the Mississippi River, and follows a general course, nearly West, across the northern part of the State of Missouri, to St. Joseph, on the Missouri River. Its entire length is two hundred and six miles.

The Lands granted to the Company are contained in alternate sections of one mile square, within a breadth of fifteen miles on each side of the road. Through some of them the road passes, and other portions vary in distance from one to fifteen miles.

At the time the grant was made by Congress, all the remaining Government Lands were fixed at a minimum price of $2.50 per acre. These were rapidly sold, and are now owned by individuals. On most of them considerable progress has been made in settlement and cultivation.

Any person now settling on the lands of the Company, will find it widely different from a new country, as at no point will neighbors be very far distant; while there are many villages and cities, ranging from a few hundred to three thousand inhabitants, all of which are rapidly increasing in size and importance.

Wherever depots are established on the road, a village at once springs up, with shops, stores, mills, etc., affording great convenience to the surrounding country.

The road was opened for use throughout its entire length, in February, 1859, and is now in successful operation, doing a large and rapidly increasing business, both in freight and passengers.

CONNECTING ROADS.

Railroads are now in progress from Palmyra to Quincy, twelve miles, and from Hannibal to Naples, forty miles. The first will afford direct Railroad communication with Chicago, and the second connecting at Naples, with the Great Western Road of Illinois, will furnish another direct communication with the East, and all States bordering on the Ohio River.

Both of these roads, it is expected, will be completed in 1859. The North Missouri Railroad is now open to Hudson, where it connects with the H. and St. Jo. Railroad, about seventy miles west of Hannibal, furnishing a railroad connection with St. Louis, which will be of great advantage during the short time navigation is suspended in the winter.

From St. Joseph, roads are projected, running north and south, and in various directions into Kansas. Some of these have liberal grants to aid in their construction, and no doubt will soon be built.

Daily lines of passenger steamboats run from St. Joseph, in connection with the Railroad, to Leavenworth and Kansas City on the south, and to Omaha and Council Bluff on the north.

PRICES AND TERMS OF PAYMENT.

The price will vary, according to quality of soil and location. Excellent Farming Lands will be sold, at prices ranging from $5 to $20 per acre, and contracts for deeds may be made, providing, that the purchase money shall be paid in nine annual installments; the first, in two years from the date of the contract. Five per cent. interest will be charged, payable yearly, in advance, the first payment of interest being made, on the day of the purchase, THUS EXTENDING THE TIME OF PAYMENT, OVER A PERIOD OF TEN YEARS, WITH ONLY FIVE PER CENT. INTEREST.

That every one may fully understand the terms proposed, we give the statement of account, with the purchaser of eighty acres of land, on the 1st of August, 1859, at ten dollars per acre, amounting to $800:

Aug. 1, 1859—Paid one year's interest on $800 at 5 per cent., and received contract for deed, ...		$40 00
" 1, 1860—Paid one year's interest as above,		40 00
" 1, 1861—Paid first installment of purchase money, being one-ninth of $800,	$88 89	
" 1, " —Paid one year's interest on balance due, $711 11, as above, .	35 55	124 44
" 1, 1862—Paid second installment, . . .	88 89	
" 1, " —Paid one year's int. on $622 22	31 11	120 00
" 1, 1863—Paid third installment, . . .	88 89	
" 1, " —Paid one year's int. on $533 33	26 66	115 55
" 1, 1864—Paid fourth installment, . . .	88 89	
" 1, " —Paid one year's int. on $444 44	22 22	111 11
" 1, 1865—Paid fifth installment, . . .	88 89	
" 1, " —Paid one year's int. on $355 55	17 78	106 67
" 1, 1866—Paid sixth installment, . . .	88 89	
" 1, " —Paid one year's int. on $266 66	13 33	102 22
" 1, 1867—Paid seventh installment, . . .	88 89	
" 1, " —Paid one year's int. on $177 77	8 89	97 78
" 1, 1868—Paid eighth installment, . . .	88 89	
" 1, " —Paid one year's int. on $88 89	4 45	93 34
" 1, 1869—Paid ninth installment, and received deed, ...		88 89
		$1040 00

The Company desire to encourage settlement upon their lands, of those who will cultivate the soil and make themselves homes, and will hold out no inducements to the mere speculator. To secure this result the purchasers on long credit, will be required to fence and cultivate, each year, for the first three years, not less than one-tenth of the land purchased. Where purchasers prefer to make payments in cash, or one-third in cash and the balance in two equal annual payments, with interest, at ten per cent., a discount will be made of twenty per cent., on the price for the long time, with low interest.

The Land Bonds of the Company will be taken in payment, and considered as cash.

This will place it in the power of persons of the most moderate means, to obtain for themselves a home, while those who have money, will find great advantage in investing it in improvements and stock.

Farmers here, well qualified to judge, express the opinion that the liberal terms of payment proposed, afford an advantage to purchasers equal to fifty per cent., added to the price of lands sold for cash.

Every judicious person seeking a home at the West, will compare the different localities, as to their adaptation to different crops, whether the soil and subsoil are such as to render them permanently productive, or otherwise—as to healthfulness of climate, and especially their position with regard to a market and the expense of transportation.

Local and temporary causes, or speculative feeling, may often in a new country, produce an unnatural activity for a time, but they can not be relied upon for permanent advancement and prosperity.

ADVANTAGES OF POSITION.

For natural advantages, this region of country stands unequaled. Its latitude is the same as the southern portion 'of Pennsylvania, giving it a climate at the same time removed from the severe cold and long winters of the North, and from the hot and relaxing influences of the South. It is widely distant both from the ocean and those immense bodies of fresh water, forming the great lakes of the interior. As a result, the air is dryer, the storms of rain are short, and it is exempt from those long and drizzly seasons of wet weather, so annoying to the farmer, in many parts of the country, while there is an abundance of rain for useful purposes.

This dryness of the atmosphere and mildness of climate render it peculiarly adapted to be the residence of those predisposed to pulmonary diseases, many of whom, rapidly recover under its influence, and become hale and robust.

IT IS EXTREMELY WELL WATERED.

A glance at the maps, shows it intersected by numerous streams, many of which afford water power. There are frequent springs, and where additional supplies are wanted for stock, the subsoil is of such a character, that pools can be easily formed which will afford an abundant supply for the entire year. Generally good wells can be obtained at from ten to thirty feet.

Persons locating in elevated places have only to dig in the earth to form a cistern, which, in most cases, even without a lining of cement, will hold an abundance of water for family use of the best character.

ROLLING AND HEALTHY.

Unlike Illinois, and much of Iowa and Wisconsin, the face of the country is quite rolling. This allows the surplus water to drain off, which would otherwise stagnate and induce disease; and, consequently, it is more healthy than Indiana and Illinois, and other places where the surface is generally level.

IT IS WELL WOODED.

Probably there is no place where fuel can not be had within a distance of from four to five miles, and, generally, an abundant supply may be found near at hand, not only for fuel but for fencing, which greatly diminishes the cost of improving a farm, and really adds several dollars per acre to its value.

SHELTER FROM THE PRAIRIE WIND.

There is another great advantage growing out of the uneven surface of the country, in connection with the supply of timber. They afford protection from the piercing winds of winter, which, sweeping over the level prairies of the west, where not a hill or a tree affords a shelter, render life there sometimes almost insupportable; and many who have made such locations without consideration, are now seeking to exchange them for those more sheltered.

Any one who has attempted to cross any lake or large pond in a boisterous winter day, can form some idea of the difficulties referred to, especially when he considers that not only the house and its inmates are thus exposed, but generally the domestic animals. Barns in the newer portions of the West are rarely found, especially where the unbroken prairie furnishes no timber for their construction.

CENTRAL POSITION.

It lies in the very heart of the United States, and of the Continent, and yet is embraced by two of the most noble Rivers of the earth; and by means of them and their tributaries, connects with an inland navigation of unequaled extent.

The Mississippi River, styled "The Father of Waters," is seldom long obstructed with ice, and affords an outlet to the Gulf, and communication with the Atlantic Ports, and the commerce of the world.

The opening of the Hannibal and St. Joseph Railroad, in connection with the natural advantages referred to, places this region in a position, unequaled by any other portion of the country.

SOIL.

BOTTOM LAND.—There is considerable variety in the soil. First, there are the bottom lands bordering the numerous streams. In other parts of the country, these would be called "Intervals" or "meadows." They are nearly level, and some of them several miles in width. The soil is a rich alluvial deposit, of great depth, and inexhaustible fertility, partially covered with wood. Though at present, these lands are not so much regarded, yet at no distant day, they will be considered among the most valuable in the country, and will produce the largest crops of hemp.

UPLAND.—The upland depends very much for its character, upon the subsoil. The vegetable mold, very rich and dark, varies in depth from one to three feet, and is often deeper. A large part of the subsoil is of a stiff, hard character, almost impervious to water, but compounded of such fertile elements, that when exposed to the action of the air, it becomes pulverized and produces almost any crop abundantly. On such soils deep plowing only is required to develop its fertility to any extent. Soil like this, will produce the most abundant crops without diminution, as is found by experience, while those based on loose material, as sand or gravel, will soon show a diminished yield, unless kept in condition by manure.

There are other soils of similar character as to the vegetable mold, where the subsoil is more porous. These are best adapted to the culture of Hemp, and produce the best Tobacco.

Occasionally the surface is too much broken for general cultivation, but this affords excellent pasture, and will be valuable for raising stock. It is also believed that Grapes will be cultivated on the slopes to great advantage, as they now are on similar land in other parts of the State.

PRODUCTIONS.

CORN is a leading article of production. Very little labor is bestowed upon its cultivation, and the average yield is not less than fifty bushels per acre, in ordinary seasons; while those who give more attention to the conditions required for a good crop, readily obtain from seventy-five to one hundred and twenty-five bushels per acre. The growth is very luxuriant, and it is not uncommon to see fields where the stalks average fifteen feet in hight.

WHEAT.—It is most admirably adapted to the culture of wheat, which succeeds best on the hill slopes and poorer soils, as it runs too much to straw, and lodges on the richest land, until cropped for a few years in corn or tobacco.

Owing to peculiarities of soil and climate, in nearly all that region, finding a market at Chicago, is cultivated the Spring Wheat. Here, Winter Wheat is raised almost exclusively, and the quality is nowhere surpassed. The advantages from this are important. In sowing and harvesting, it interferes less with other crops. It comes into market in time to secure the highest prices usually paid for NEW WHEAT. The yield per acre is from three to five bushels more than Spring Wheat, while the market price is greater on the different varieties, from ten to over forty cents per bushel, and may be considered as averaging fully twenty-five cents advance.

OTHER GRAINS, POTATOES, ETC.—For the culture of Oats, Rye, Barley, and other crops, usually raised in the more Northern States, this region is well adapted, and large returns are realized.

The common, and also sweet potatoes, are produced abundantly. Flax does remarkably well, and two tons of hay to the acre, is but an ordinary crop.

HEMP.—Hemp is less exhausting to the soil than almost any other crop, and may be cultivated indefinitely without manure.

Instances can easily be cited, where it has been grown upon the same land for fifteen or twenty years, with undiminished success. The profits of this crop after paying all expense of cultivation, average $20 to $25 per acre, and are often twice that amount.

Good hemp lands near the rivers are now held at from $50 to $100 per acre by the farmers; and the opening of the Railroad will soon make much of the similar land along the line of equal value.

Diminished cost of transportation, and the introduction of machinery to perform the operation of breaking, will add largely to the profits heretofore realized from this crop.

TOBACCO.—This crop is already extensively cultivated, and with great success. The lands of Macon county are considered equal to the best in Kentucky and Virginia for its production. Many other localities along the line of road are not inferior to this.

Less care has been bestowed upon this crop than its importance deserves, and, consequently, the article sent to market is not usually of the best quality; still the ordinary net profits have been from $25 to $30 per acre.

To give an idea of the profits sometimes realized, we will state that the ordinary yield is 1,000 pounds per acre, but often reaches 1,600 and 2,000 pounds, and even 2,100 pounds is obtained.

The crop of 1856 sold in Hannibal, at an average of ten cents per pound, although an average price for ten years, has been nearer six cents. This would make the production of an acre sometimes exceed $200.

It may be cultivated by men of small means, as no outlay of capital is required, and much of the labor can be done by children. One man will cultivate five acres in tobacco besides sufficient of other crops to support his family.

This crop is more exhausting to the soil, but is followed well by wheat. The manure of the farm should be saved and applied to the tobacco field. This, with "rotation," keeps the land in good condition.

It always sells for cash, and the traders say "Tobacco growers are good paymasters."

STOCK RAISING.

Probably no part of the country affords equal advantages for the rearing of stock.

There are still extensive ranges of the richest pasture, with abundance of water and wood to shelter from heat and storms. The bottoms furnish feed both earlier and later than the uplands, and the short mild winters require but little provision for their support. The difference between Missouri and other States is very material, as shown by the census returns of 1850. If we consider eight sheep as equal to one cow, in the hay consumed, and add the returns of horses, mules, oxen, cows, and other cattle, we find the following result:

STATES.	TONS OF HAY.	NO. OF ANIMALS.	NO. OF LBS. TO EACH.
Missouri,	116,925	1,153,810'	202
Iowa,	89,025	194,656	915
Illinois,	601,952	1,302,017	925
Michigan,	404,934	426,377	1,899
Wisconsin,	275,662	229,380	2,404
Maine,	755,889	441,562	3,424
Massachusetts,	651,807	325,825	4,001

This shows conclusively the superiority of Missouri for stock growing.

Farmers here are turning their attention to it with great success, and consider it the most profitable branch of their business.

Intelligent gentlemen from the older States are already purchasing large tracts of land and making liberal outlays of money to engage in this pursuit.

SWINE.

The growth of swine is greatly promoted by the mast of the forest; and the abundant crops of corn make the fattening process comparatively cheap. Both cattle and swine are extensively raised at present, and with large profits.

FRUIT.

Every one seeking to make a HOME will wish to supply himself with fruit. Here, all those of temperate climates perfectly luxuriate. The growth of apples, both for quantity and quality, is truly marvelous; some are found weighing two pounds or more, and without a blemish. Plums grow wild, and are easily cultivated. Peaches and melons can not be surpassed. Grapes are indigenous, and, in some sections, are cultivated for the manufacture of wine, and found very profitable. They are easily raised by open culture.

The growth of fruit not only affords many cheap luxuries, but may also be made a source of very considerable profit.

LUMBER AND BUILDING MATERIALS.

There is no white pine in Missouri, but a supply of hard wood and various kinds of soft—as Cottonwood, Sycamore, Lind, etc.—can be had at convenient points, and generally at moderate prices. At Hannibal, Pine lumber is brought from the upper Mississippi, and sold at reasonable rates. Here, also, are mills for dressing lumber; and material can be provided for the erection of buildings, requiring only to be put together; or houses can be erected by contract, of any desired style.

Materials for brick are generally abundant, and the stone and fuel are always at hand for burning lime.

READY MADE COTTAGES.

Arrangements have been made with responsible parties, to furnish, delivered on the cars at Hannibal, readymade cottages of a variety of styles, at a cost varying from $125 to $300, according to the size and style of finish; and so complete in every respect, as to require but four or five days after their delivery upon the ground, to be ready for the occupancy of a family.

FENCING.

Fencing must usually be done to protect against swine, and rails will generally be used. If the purchaser secures a portion of timber land, he has only to add his labor, and a substantial fence can be built at a cost of from fifty cents to one dollar per rod.

Of course the same facilities exist here as elsewhere for hedging, but the success of this is quite doubtful.

The cost of a substantial post and board fence in any prairie country at the West is from $1.50 to $2.00 per rod. Most of this is for materials, and must be paid for in cash at the outset, which is a great drawback upon the settler with limited means, and when built it is neither as good or durable as a fence of rails. This is one great advantage to be realized from the supply of timber over Illinois and Iowa, and the territory west of the Missouri River, where lumber is generally very scarce.

COAL.

Coal abounds on many parts of tor line of road, and, probably, underlies the whole country.

In the report of the Geological Survey of the State, by Prof. Swallow, it is estimated that within fifteen miles of the Hannibal and St. Joseph Railroad, and within the counties of Macon, Linn, Livingston and Chariton alone, there is not less than 1,500 square miles of coal fields, containing workable coal, after allowing one-half for waste, equal to 9,000,000 tuns.

Other counties will also furnish large quantities.

Under the influence of the road, mining is just being com-

2

menced; and, though the operations are still very imperfect, coal is obtained at prices making it cheaper fuel than the mere preparation of wood.

There can be no doubt that mining will furnish employment for a large population.

MANUFACTURES.

At the Iron Mountain, in Missouri, it is estimated that the cost of producing the pig-iron is less than in any other part of the country. So rich, in fact, is the ore, that it may be made into "blooms," with no intermediate process.

By the recent opening of the Iron Mountain Railroad, for three dollars per tun, iron is now taken from the mines to St. Louis, where are mills for rolling, and the article is extensively manufactured.

The cheapness of iron, the supply of lumber, the abundance of coal, and its position with reference to the yet undeveloped portions of our country, indicate Missouri as a most favorable location for extensive manufactures; and very considerable progress has already been made in that direction.

TOWN LOTS.

Stations have been established along the line of the road, at various points, from five to ten miles apart, around which flourishing villages are springing up, in most of which the Railroad Company have an interest, where eligible locations can be obtained, on favorable terms, by the mechanic, manufacturer, or trader.

The growth of some of these has been remarkably rapid. Where, two years since, nothing was to be seen but the unbroken prairie, villages of from 300 to 800 inhabitants now meet the eye; churches have been built; schools established; stores and mechanics' shops are in successful operation; and everything indicates an activity and prosperity which can only be the result of industry and enterprise, rightly directed in developing the wealth of a country unsurpassed by any in the salubrity of its climate, and the fertility of its soil.

MISSOURI FARMER'S HOME IN 1859.

EDUCATION.

Liberal provisions have been made by Missouri for popular instruction, affording free schools to all her children, with only a light tax, and in many cases none at all.

The principal obstacle in the practical working of her system, is the difficulty of obtaining good instructors, and perhaps there is no State where there is greater demand, or where they could secure higher compensation.

To show more fully the provisions made for education, we insert a communication from the Hon. WILLIAM CARSON, of Palmyra, a Senator, and one who has ever felt a deep interest in this subject. He says:

"It should be a subject of deep concern to every one settling in a country, to know the provisions for educational purposes, and the disposition of the government and people to educate the rising generation.

"Missouri has not been unmindful of this great and interesting subject. The wise and good men who formed her Constitution, incorporated in her fundamental law this provision, (Art. vi, Sec. 1,) 'THAT SCHOOLS AND THE MEANS OF EDUCATION SHALL FOREVER BE ENCOURAGED IN THIS STATE.'

"In accordance with this provision, and to carry out its beneficent purpose, the Legislature, in 1838–9, adopted a common school system, taking that of New York as a model, and modifying it to suit the different circumstances existing here. This system has been in successful operation since.

"To support these schools, the State has a fund amounting to near seven hundred thousand dollars, denominated the State School Fund; to this is to be added the money derived from the sale of the 16th section in each township, called the Township School Fund; and all fines and forfeitures, called the County School Fund. We have not the means of ascertaining the precise amount of the Township and County School Funds in the State, which vary in different counties, according to the price at which the sixteenth sections were sold; but we have endeavored to approximate as nearly as possible, from the data we have.

" In the county of Marion (in which Hannibal is situated), the fund amounts to $36,072. There are in the State one hundred and six organized counties, and, taking Marion as an average, the aggregate amount of Township and County School Funds in the State is $3,823,632. Add to this the State School Fund, $672,000, and it shows the total School Fund, from these sources, to be $4,495,632.

" Or it may be arrived at in this way: It will be seen by inspecting Colton's Map for 1854, that there are in the State 1900 sixteenth sections, which, multiplied by 640, the number of acres in a section, gives 1,216,000 acres, which, estimated at the low price of four dollars per acre, would make the sum of $4,864,000, which, added to the State Fund, would make the total $5,536,000, or about one million more than to take the county of Marion as an average, as above. We think, then, that we may safely set down the State, County and Township Fund at four and one-half millions. To these is still to be added the 'Swamp Land Fund,' which will certainly amount to $1,000,000, and we have the total aggregate, in round numbers, of five and one-half millions, sacredly devoted to the cause of common school education, the interest of which only is annually distributed; but besides this, twenty-five per cent. of the annually accruing revenue, amounting to about $150,000, is distributed for the same praiseworthy object. In several of the counties along the line of the road, the 'Swamp Land Fund' will be very large, and, taken altogether, in many counties, the income will be quite sufficient to keep up 'Free Schools' the whole year, thus affording gratuitous instruction to every child. In every county, Free Schools are now kept part of the year. In addition to the foregoing, there are nine regularly chartered Colleges in the State, and a large number of 'High Schools,' (over forty, it is believed,) for both males and females; and, in addition to all these, the State has a University, with an endowment fund of one hundred thousand dollars, and a spacious and beautiful edifice, sufficient to accommodate from four to six hundred students. It is in successful operation, having an able faculty, consisting of a president and seven professors.

"This is located at Columbia, in Boone county, near the center of the State, and within fifty miles of the Hannibal and St. Joseph Railroad.

"While speaking of the institutions of learning in Missouri, it may not be considered invidious if we refer more particularly and definitely to some of them situated in the countries through which the road passes. St. Paul's (Episcopal) College is situated at Palmyra, fourteen miles from Hannibal, immediately on the line of the road, and is, therefore, easily accessible, from almost every direction, by the railroad or by the river. The College has beautiful grounds and buildings, affording ample accommodations for a large number of students, and has obtained a very high reputation for thoroughness in instruction and discipline. There is also, at Palmyra, the Presbyterian Female Institute, a Seminary of high character; and the Baptists have a Male and Female Seminary, which has been in successful operation for several years, and was chartered by the last Legislature as a College. For beauty and healthfulness of location, and moral and refined society, Palmyra is perhaps not surpassed by any other town in the State.

"McGee College (male and female), under the patronage of the Cumberland Presbyterian Church, is situated near the line of the road, in Macon county, and has attained considerable reputation as a literary institute. It has a beautiful and healthy location in the country, and has buildings to accommodate a large number of students.

"From this it will be seen that Missouri has educational resources and facilities equal to the most favored of the new States, and far in advance of some of the older States.

"Emigrants may, therefore, be assured, from the foregoing facts, that in settling in Missouri, they make no sacrifice for want of the means and facilities for educating their children. These, to a great extent, are already provided, and in successful operation."

MARKETS.

The location of this region gives it great advantages in easy and cheap communication with all the markets, not only of this country, but of the world. Large quantities of fruit, sweet potatoes, and tobacco will be sent to those States further north, where these crops either can not be raised, or to but little advantage. It borders upon the territories, where production is still below the demand for consumption, owing to the immense emigration. Here provisions will naturally be made for trading-parties to Santa Fe—the American Fur Company—the travel across the plains, and the wants of the General Government in sustaining its military posts and operations, which all combine to furnish a most desirable market. Bordering upon the Lower Mississippi and the Gulf, is the immense planting region of our country, which cultivating mainly the leading staples, makes large drafts upon the more northern States for the means of subsistence. For all this, the region under consideration is most favorably situated.

Missouri extends to nearly the northern limit of uninterrupted steam navigation on the Mississippi. The rapids immediately above, at all times, obstruct and increase the cost of navigation, and, for a considerable portion of the year, interrupt it entirely. The obstructions from ice are also much less here than above. Boats usually run every month in the year, and some winters without any interruption; while further north the river is closed for months. This naturally makes St. Louis the primary market for those productions designed for the south, or the eastern seaboard, as well as for those who seek a foreign port directly from New Orleans.

It is well known that Chicago is the largest primary grain market in the country, receiving its supplies not only from Illinois, but from Iowa and Wisconsin. Below will be found tables showing the prices of leading articles of produce in each month for the year 1857, both in Chicago and St. Louis. These have been carefully compiled from the daily Commercial Letters and Reports of Board of Trade, and are believed to be reliable. Had we been able to obtain the data, these tables would have embraced the report of other years, but this would not probably have altered the comparative results.

Monthly Statement of the amount of Wheat received in St. Louis in 1857, with the Average Price of different varieties.

MONTHS.	NO. OF BUSHELS.	AV. PRICE SPRING	AV. PRICE FALL RED.	AV. PRICE WHITE.
January............	18,414	100 @ 105	107 @ 118	115 @ 120
February...........	223,052	100 " 108	109 " 116	115 " 130
March.............	315,041	109 " 115	117 " 125	127 " 136
April..............	342.587	102 " 113	126 " 131	146 " 150
May...............	375,008	120 " 134	148 " 156	165 " 180
June..............	372,448	109 " 124	139 " 149	156 " 163
July..............	111,372	101 " 119	127 " 142	145 " 151
August............	243.603	97 " 108	107 " 115	124 " 135
September.........	242.267	73 " 86	92 " 104	118 " 128
October...........	139,555	61 " 73	70 " 98	90 " 104
November.........	225,846	76 " 84	86 " 104	111 " 117
December..........	274.285	61 " 79	85 " 107	104 " 117
Total........	2,883,548			

Monthly Statement of the amount of Wheat received in Chicago in 1857, with the Average Price of different varieties.

MONTHS.	NO. OF BUSHELS.	AV. PRICE SPRING.	AV. PRICE FALL RED.	AV. PRICE WHITE.
January...........	114,636	86 @ 89	101 @ 104	110 @ 115
February.........	171,382	81 " 89	101 " 104	113 " 117
March............	355,701	88 " 88	103 " 105	118 " 122
April.............	141.347	90 " 91	103 " 107	125 " 129
May	317,717	117 " 118	128 " 132	145 " 148
June.............	682,918	122 " 123	135 " 135	150 " 150
July	397.046	119 " 121	" 135	" 150
August...........	894,227	108 " 109	121 " 122	139 " 141
September.........	2,806,226	78 " 80	99 " 101	111 " 112
October	2,462.025	67 " 70	67 " 80	NONE
November.........	2,510,318	59 " 62	62 " 72	IN
December..........	168,741	54 " 57	55 " 75	MARKET.
Total........	11,002.284			

Table of Monthly Prices of Corn and Oats at Chicago and St. Louis, with the quantity received for 1857.

MONTHS.	IN CHICAGO.		IN ST. LOUIS.	
	CORN.	OATS.	CORN.	OATS.
January..........	39 @ 40¾	35½ @ 35	57½ @ 62½	NONE.
February.........	38¼ " 40	37½ " 38	54 " 57	52 @ 56½
March............	34 " 38¾	37¼ " 38¼	52 " 59	55 " 56
April............	46 " 46¼	44 " 45	55 " 57	58 " 64
May..............	65½ " 66¼	58½ " 60	68 " 84	68 " 76
June.............	65¾ " 64¼	57½ " 58½	70½ " 85½	67 " 70
July.............	66 " 66	55 " 54	66 " 77½	64 " 68
August...........	68 " 68½	46½ " 48	66 " 75	43 " 53
September........	54 " 55	26 " 27½	57 " 66½	33 " 38
October..........	48 " 49	26 " 26½	54 " 65	35 " 42
November.........	44 " 46	24 " 24½	44½ " 55	33 " 38
December.........	43½ " 43¼	23½ " 24	37 " 42½	27 " 31
Total rec'ts in bush.	6,667,324	474,290	2,485,786	845,295

Table showing the Average Price of Tobacco and Hemp at St. Louis, in each month, for the year 1857.

MONTHS.	HEMP PER TON.	TOBACCO, SHIP. ⅌ CWT.
January..............	$160.00 @ $170.00	NO QUOTATIONS.
February	156.00 " 164.00	$10.00 @ $15.00
March................	120.00 " 136.00	10.00 " 17.00
April	119.00 " 134.00	12.00 " 17.25
May	121.00 " 135.00	13.00 " 19.00
June.................	120.00 " 128.00	10.00 " 16.00
July.................	120.00 " 134.00	8.50 " 14.00
August	116.00 " 129.00	8.00 " 15.50
September	93.00 " 110.50	8.00 " 12.00
October	70.00 " 85.00	NO QUOTATIONS.
November.............	70.00 " 81.00	DO.
December	75.00 " 88.00	7.00 @ 9.00

From the foregoing it appears that the average of prices in St. Louis, for 1857, was greater than those in Chicago, as follows: 11 cents per bushel on wheat, nearly 11 cents per bushel on corn, and over 11 cents per bushel on oats, and the average difference between Spring and Red Fall Wheat was 15 cents, and White Fall 32 cents per bushel, being two cents greater in St. Louis than in Chicago. When we consider that the great majority in Chicago market is Spring, and in St. Louis Fall Wheat, it will be safe to estimate that the farmers who market at the latter place, receive 30 cents per bushel more for their wheat than those who market at Chicago. This will at least hold true of all raised in Missouri, where Spring Wheat is seldom cultivated.

The reason for this difference in price is obvious. Chicago has but one outlet for its provisions, and that the Eastern seaboard, the water communication with which, is obstructed by ice, for about five months in the year, which naturally brings prices to the lowest points, at that season most convenient for the farmer to market his crops, so that he must either submit to winter rates, or hold until the Spring, and take to market when his farm work is most pressing.

On the other hand, St. Louis has a large and profitable market from which Chicago is shut out; and as ice seldom obstructs the navigation, can at all times forward produce to the Atlantic Ports, at less than the summer water rates from Chicago.

This fact will be made more apparent by the following statement:

COMPARISON BETWEEN CHICAGO AND ST. LOUIS IN THE COST OF FREIGHT TO NEW YORK.

Extremely low summer water rates from Chicago to New York are fifty cents per hundred pounds, and in ordinary produce, the weight rather than the bulk controls the price. This would make the cost of transportation on a bushel of wheat, or corn, 30 cents, on a barrel of Flour, $1.08, and on a barrel of Pork, $1.65.

3

From St. Louis to New York produce is taken by the largest class of River Steamboats to New Orleans, where sailing vessels carry it the remaining distance. In these vessels, bulk controls the expense of carriage, more than weight, so that flour or pork goes at less price per tun than grain.

Moderate prices between these ports are :

Freight on Grain, per bushel,   .   .   . $0.25
"   " Flour, " bbl., ...   80
"   " Pork and Beef, per bbl.,   .   . 1.00

But it must be borne in mind that the river below St. Louis is seldom obstructed by ice, while from Chicago, water navigation is interrupted for nearly five months in the year, when forwarders are obliged to pay Railroad rates of fare.

These were placed unusually low in the winter of 1857–58, and were as follows :

Flour per barrel, to New York,   .   .   . $1.55
Grain " bushel   "   .   .   .   50
Pork and Beef, per bbl. "   .   .   .   2.75

In consideration of the length of time navigation is suspended at Chicago, it will be fair to add to the water rates of freight at least one-fifth of the difference between these and the winter rates, to obtain a fair estimate of the average cost of transportation. This gives us from Chicago :

Freight on Grain, per bushel,   .   .   . $0.34
"   " Flour, " bbl. 1.17
"   " Beef and Pork, per bbl.,   .   . 1.87

An ordinary Railroad freight would be 8 cents per bushel on grain, and 15 cents per 100 lbs. on Flour and packed meats, for every hundred miles.

The lands now offered are at an average distance from Hannibal of about one hundred miles.

The opening of the line of Railroad has the effect, to make very depot a market, and the competition among the buyers will fetch the prices nearly up to those of the principal markets, less the cost of transportation.

Now, to ascertain the comparative value of land in different localities at the West, we will estimate the value of a crop on a farm of 160 acres, on the Hannibal and St. Joseph Railroad, 100 miles from Hannibal, on a similar farm 100 miles from Chicago in any direction, and on one near Iowa City, in Iowa, 250 miles from Chicago, by the Rock Island Railroad. If we allow 60 acres for the various purposes of the family, we have 100 acres on which to raise a crop for market; which we will suppose is fifty acres in Corn, and fifty in Wheat.

The average yield in Iowa, and Northern Illinois, will be 22 bushels of Spring wheat per acre, and 50 bushels of corn. In Missouri, 25 bushels of Winter wheat per acre, and 50 bushels of corn.

If now we assume the prices in New York to be 75 cents per bushel on corn, $1.25 on Spring wheat, and $1.50 on Winter wheat, and estimate the freight from Hannibal to St. Louis at five cents per bushel, we shall have the basis of calculation.

From the point, 100 miles west of Hannibal, the freight would be to Hannibal 8 cents, to St. Louis 5 cents, and to New York 25 cents, making 38 cents; reducing the price of corn to 37 cents, and of Winter wheat to $1.12 per bushel.

From the farm, 100 miles from Chicago, the freight would be 8 cents to Chicago, and to New York 34 cents, making 42 cents per bushel; and reducing the price of corn to 33 cents, and of Spring wheat to 83 cents per bushel.

From the farm, near Iowa city, the freight would be 20 cents to Chicago, and to New York 34 cents, making in all 54 cents per bushel; reducing the price of corn to 21 cents, and Spring wheat to 71 cents per bushel.

We have then the following results:

Farm in Missouri, 100 miles from Hannibal.

2,500 bushels corn, at 37 cents,	. .	$925
1,250 " Winter wheat, at $1.12,	.	1,400
Amounting to, ...		$2,325

Farm in Illinois, 100 miles from Chicago.

2,500 bushels corn, at 33 cents,	. .	$825
1,100 " Spring wheat, at 83 cents,	.	913
Amounting to,	. . . . .	$1,738

Farm near Iowa City, in Iowa.

2,500 bushels corn, at 21 cents,	. .	$525
1,100 " Spring wheat, at 71 cents,	.	781
Amounting to,	. . . . .	$1,306

Hence it appears that the income from a grain farm of 160 acres, 100 miles from Hannibal, in Missouri, is greater than that from a similar farm in Illinois, 100 miles from Chicago, by $587; and than that from a farm near Iowa City, by $1,019. Any one may easily estimate what effect this should have upon the value of the lands at the different localities.

From the rates of freight before given, it is apparent that if the production of the farms considered, should be converted into Pork, Beef, or Flour, the difference of freight would be still more against the farms in Illinois and Iowa.

If this result is not at present strictly correct in fact, it is owing to local and temporary causes, and must inevitably be realized whenever the more complete settlement of the country obliges all surplus products to seek an Eastern market—a time certainly not very far distant.

At the present time, produce in Kansas is much higher than in Illinois; but with the increase of population, in a few years, supply will greatly exceed demand, and the surplus will then have to seek the same market, when the order of prices will be reversed.

The intelligent farmer, seeking for himself a HOME, will not consider so much what he can make by fortuitous circumstances and speculation, as what region has really the most substantial advantages, on which to build a permanent and healthy growth.

In the comparison drawn, we have supposed the farms considered devoted to grain; but this is by no means the most

profitable crop in Missouri. Hemp and Tobacco pay much larger profits; and stock growing, for those who have the required capital, is better than either. The farmers of this region, with ordinary industry and prudence, are rapidly growing rich.

HANNIBAL.

The city of Hannibal is beautifully situated on the west bank of the Mississippi, at the terminus of the Hannibal and St. Joseph Railroad, and is the commercial depot for an extensive district of country, extending west of St. Joseph. The Pike County Railroad, and the Hannibal and Peoria Railroad, now in process of construction, and the Mississippi Valley Railroad projected, will radiate from this point, while the Mississippi river unites with them in bearing into her lap the profits of a large inland commerce. Hannibal is the lumber depot for North Missouri and Kansas, and the point where all western emigrants can obtain their outfits on most favorable terms. It has a population of about 8000, and, from its present rapid progress, seems destined soon to obtain an importance second to few cities in the west. Various manufacturing interests are already permanently developed, and every branch of industry is bountifully rewarded, while the present prices of real estate are such as to offer favorable inducements for the investment of capital.

ST. JOSEPH.

The city of St. Joseph, the western terminus of this great road, is upon the Missouri river, which is navigable for two thousand miles above that city. At St. Joseph will converge that grand network of railroads, which will, in another generation, cover the territories of Kansas and Nebraska, and in its market will be exchanged the manufactures and luxuries of the east, for the beef, wool, hides, and golden corn of the immense country lying between the Missouri river and the

Pacific slope of the Rocky Mountain chain, which divides the waters of the two great oceans. Here, beyond all question, will be a large commercial city, and all kinds of produce will find a ready and profitable market. There being no navigable waters west of the Missouri, and no point where the railroad system of the mighty west can again concentrate, all reasoning men must at once see the magnificent future of this young Queen of the Missouri.

ST. LOUIS.

St. Louis will be the principal market where those supplies which every family needs will be obtained for this region of country; and her facilities enable her to supply the smaller trades on better terms than any other western city.

The heavier articles, as salt, coffee, sugar, and molasses, are obtained from New Orleans, where the former articles are directly imported, and the latter are produced; and her railroad connections with all the commercial ports of the east, enable her to supply the lighter articles of commerce, at moderate prices. She is also taking a leading position in manufactures, for which she has great facilities, and many articles will be furnished from her own shops, of superior quality. Already her population exceeds 140,000, and is rapidly increasing. When we look at the resources of the country tributary to her, which is yet to be developed, it is manifest she must soon become the largest inland city on the continent.

The neighborhood of a large and growing city, with extensive manufactures, and accumulation of capital, can not fail to have a favorable effect upon the producing industry of the country.

TRADERS AND MECHANICS.

It is hardly necessary to say, that in a country filling with population, with cities and villages rapidly growing up, there

will be abundant employment for all in the different branches
of mechanics, and also desirable openings for trade.

The surplus earnings, carefully invested in land, soon
secures an independence.

ADVANTAGES FROM SETTLING IN NORTH-MISSOURI.

To enumerate some of the advantages of locating on the
lands now offered for sale, we may say that the climate is
healthful, and removed from the extremes of heat and cold;
the winter short; the air pure and salubrious; the soil of an
unlimited fertility, with a retentive subsoil, containing the
most fertilizing properties; there are numerous streams and
springs; while the rolling surface secures drainage, and pre-
vents stagnation. The great majority is prairie, ready at
once for the plow, with sufficient wood for fuel, fence, and
shelter. Coal is also abundant to supply any deficiency, and
afford means of profitable employment in mining, and with
other important minerals, naturally leads to manufactures.
All the productions of temperate climates are abundant. It
is peculiarly adapted to winter wheat, which probably adds
from $5 to $10 per acre to the value of the wheat crop, over
sections growing the spring varieties. All grains find a much
better market at St. Louis than is afforded at Chicago.

Much of the soil is well adapted to the culture of Hemp,
Tobacco and the Grape, which are very profitable, and can
not be grown successfully in a higher latitude. For stock
raising, in all its branches, it can hardly be equaled; and its
water navigation, seldom interrupted by ice, enables its products to find a market easily in all directions, at home or
abroad; while its central position, and the ease with which it
can communicate with the proposed routes for the Pacific
Railroad, either North or South, together with the fact that
the Hannibal and St. Joseph Road will reach the Missouri
river years in advance of any other line, render it nearly
certain that this must form a part of that great channel of
communication, to be extended to the Pacific, over which will

THE CLIMATE is temperate and salubrious, as we might expect in a high rolling country under that latitude. The winters are short and mild, while the summers are long and warm.

SOIL.—Nearly all the soil of this region is based upon the fine silicious marl of the Bluff Formation. As this fact would indicate, they possess all the good qualities of the very best Western soils. Those in the valleys of the streams are not inferior in fertility to the very best alluvial soils. But those upon the ridges and knobs are of a lighter character, and much inferior for the ordinary uses of the farmer. It is, how-ever, very probable, that these soils will be more valuable for the cultivation of the grape, than even our richest soils for the ordinary purposes of agriculture; for the grape will succeed on the poorer ridges, when the soil has the proper composition.

A more careful examination of this part of the lands of the Company, will enable us to decide this point with certainty, as it is already proved that our climate and some of our poorer soils, are all that can be desired for the grape. Thus it will be seen, that the lands of your Company are located in one of the richest and most desirable regions of the West. The soil is scarcely surpassed in any region of equal extent, and yet the country is high, undulating, well watered, and salubrious. It is so divided into timber and prairie, as will render the opening of farms most convenient and profitable. The prairie is ready for the plow, and the best of timber at hand for build-ings and fences.

COAL.—But the vast coal beds beneath the soil give these lands a value far above all ordinary prices. According to Major Hawn's Surveys, a large portion of these lands contain at least fine workable beds of good coal. These beds will con-tain an aggregate thickness of fifteen feet, which will yield not less than 20,000 tons per acre. The coal alone, at only one cent per tun, is worth $200 per acre.

It is not possible to specify the precise extent of these coal beds, or all the lands which they underlie, until we shall have made a more careful examination of that part of the State; but it is certain that they extend under a portion of all the counties on the line of the road west of Macon.

BUILDING MATERIAL.—Good limestone, suitable for all building purposes, is abundant along the line of the road. Clays of excellent quality for common and fine brick and pottery, are found in large quantities.

WATER POWER.—The numerous streams which pass through this region, afford a large amount of water power, and many good sites for mills and factories. For a more detailed account of this region, I would refer you to the Second Annual Report of the Missouri Survey. Wishing you success in the prosecution of your great work, I remain,

Your Ob't Serv't,

G. C. SWALLOW,

State Geologist of Missouri.

We here insert various extracts from the published Report of Prof. SWALLOW and his assistants on the Geological Survey of the State:

RIVER BOTTOMS.

We have on these two streams alone (the Mississippi and Missouri) about 2,000,000 acres of the most productive and inexhaustible lands in the world, based upon the alluvial strata of sand, clay, marl, and humus; and beside, this quantity is constantly increasing, by the silting up of the lakes and sloughs.

The rich productive power of this formation is abundantly proved by the immense burden of timber growing upon it, and by the unparalleled crops of corn and hemp harvested from its cultivated fields.

The Bottom Prairie is, so far as my observation here extended, about half as extensive as the Alluvial Bottom on the same streams.

This estimate will give us about 1,000,000 acres of these vastly rich Savannas, all prepared by Nature for the plow. Their agricultural capacities are scarcely inferior to any in the world, as is abundantly demonstrated by the mineral contents of the strata, and the products of the numerous farms located upon it.

The alluvium of our river bottoms generally produces a light rich, silicious soil, which sustains a larger growth of timber than any other in the State. This variety of soil occupies the bottoms of all our large streams, covering an area of some four or five millions of acres. It is not surpassed in fertility by any in the State, and is peculiarly adapted to corn and hemp. It is usually so light and porous, and deep, that in wet weather the superabundance of water readily passes off; while in drought, the roots sink deep, and the water below easily ascends by capillary attraction, and keeps the surface moist. These scientific deductions are abundantly sustained by the experience of the unprecedented drought of the present season; as the cornfields on this soil suffered comparatively little injury from it.

BLUFF FORMATION.

This formation when well developed, usually presents a fine, pulverulent, absolutely stratified mass of light grayish bluff, silicious and slightly indurated marl. It is often penetrated by numerous tubes or cylinders, about the size or thickness of pipestems, some larger and others smaller. These phenomena have been minutely investigated, not merely as interesting scientific facts, but also as one of the most useful agricultural features of this preëminently valuable formation; for upon it, and sustained by its absolutely inexhaustible fertilizing resources, rest the very best farms of the Mississippi and Missouri valley. These tubes and holes also constitute THE MOST THOROUGH SYSTEM OF DRAINAGE imaginable.

This formation forms the upper stratum beneath the soil of

all the high lands, both timber and prairie, of all the counties north of the Osage and Missouri Rivers.*

The Bluff, when well developed, produces a light, deep calcareo-silicious soil, of the very best quality. The alumina, silex, and lime are mingled in such proportions with the other fertilizing properties in this formation, as to adapt it in an admirable degree, to the formation of soils and subsoils; and, as might be expected, the soils formed upon it under favorable circumstances, are equal to any in the country. The deleterious effects usually produced by the coal measures are prevented by the thick bluff deposit, which covers nearly all the coal strata in this State; and, indeed, the very best soils of the State overlie the coal measures.

COAL.

Mineral coal has done much to promote the rapid progress of the present century. Commerce and Manufactures could not have reached their present unprecedented prosperity without its aid. And no people can expect success in those departments of human industry, unless their territory furnishes an abundance of this useful mineral. Previous to the present survey, it was known that coal existed in many counties of the State; but there was no definite knowledge of the continuation of workable beds over any considerable area. But since the survey commenced, the Southeastern outcrop of the coal measures has been traced from the mouth of the Des Moines, through Clark, Lewis, Marion, Monroe, Audrian, Boone, Cooper, Pettis, Henry, St. Clair, Bates, and Jasper, into the Indian Territory; from Glasgow up the Missouri River to the Iowa line; and from St. Joseph along the line of the Hannibal and St. Joseph Railroad to Shelby, showing the existence of the coal measures over an area of more than 26,000 square miles, in the Northern and Western parts of the State.

---

* This embraces the entire region traversed by the Hannibal and St. Joseph Railroad.

The thickest of these beds varies from five to six feet; and, altogether, they will furnish twelve or fourteen feet of good coal. These beds extend over an area, all within fifteen miles of the Hannibal and St. Joseph Railroad, of at least 500 square miles in Macon, 400 in Linn, 400 in Livingston, and 200 in Chariton, making in all 1500 square miles, within fifteen miles of the road in these four counties alone. It is estimated by the best mining engineers of England, that every foot of workable coal will furnish 1,000,000 tuns per square mile, which would give us for these four counties 1,500,000,000 tuns for every foot in these beds. If we deduct one-half of the thickness for waste, and for the areas, where some of these beds may run out, we shall have 9,000,000,000 tuns of workable coal within the limits above mentioned, seeking transportation to the Mississippi and Missouri Rivers.

Should the road be able to transport 100,000 tuns per day, it would supply freight for 90,000 days, and allowing 300 mining days per annum, it would occupy it 300 years. At 50,000 tuns per day, it would freight the road 600 years, which is quite as long as the stockholders need provide for themselves and their heirs; as by that time Young America will have no use for Railroads.

Shelby county will also furnish small quantities; and all the counties on the line west of Livingston, have still more coal, but its depth below the surface may prevent profitable mining at the present prices of coal and labor.

But few, if any, Railroads run through so good a body of land as the Hannibal and St. Joseph. The facilities afforded by the road will bring this land into market, and settle it with a stirring agricultural population, unless speculators place its price above that of other lands possessing similar qualities and advantages.

Coal mining will also bring in an increase of population to swell the travel over this road.

VIEW OF GRAND RIVER VALLEY, FROM UTICA.

IRON.

Among minerals, Iron stands preëminent in its influence upon the power and prosperity of a nation. Nations who possess it in large quantities, and by whom it is extensively manufactured, seem to partake of its hardy nature and sterling qualities. Missouri possesses an inexhaustible supply of the very best ores of this metal. She has all the facilities for becoming the great iron mart of the Western Continent.

SPECULAR OXIDE.—This is probably the most abundant and valuable ore in the State. Iron Mountain is the largest mass observed. The hight of the mountain is 228 feet, and its base covers an area of 500 acres, which gives, according to Dr. LITTON, 1,655,280,000 cubic feet, or 230,187,375 tuns of ore. But this is only a fraction of the ore at this locality.

THE SPECULAR AND MAGNETIC OXIDES.— At Shepherd Mountain the ore is usually a mixture of these varieties, in a very pure state. The ore at this mountain exists in vertical veins, ranging in different directions through the porphyry of which the mountain is composed. They vary in thickness from one foot to fourteen. Three of these have been partially explored. They yield an enormous amount of ore.

SILICIOUS SPECULAR OXIDE.—Pilot Knob, which is of this variety, is 581 feet high, and covers an area of 360 acres. A large portion of this mountain is pure ore. The quantity is enormous, and may be considered inexhaustible. The amount above the surface can not be less than 13,972,773 tuns. But it evidently far exceeds this estimate.

There is ore enough of the very best quality within a few miles of Pilot Knob and Iron Mountain, above the surface of the valleys to furnish 1,000,000 tuns per annum of manufactured iron, for the next two hundred years.

All of these ores are well adapted to the manufacture of pig metal; and those of Iron Mountain and Shepherd Mountain, are used for making blooms by the Catalan process, in the bloomeries at Pilot Knob and Valle Forge.

LUMBER AND WATER-POWER.

It may be a matter of surprise to some to learn that Missouri, notwithstanding our heavy importation of lumber, has a great abundance of almost every desirable variety, most advantageously situated. Indeed, with the exception of white pine, cedar, and live oak, our supply seems to be all that could be desired.

On the borders of our navigable streams and their large tributaries, oak, hickory, walnut, maple, ash, linden, cherry, locust, and birch grow in the greatest abundance, and in magnificent dimensions. It seems unnecessary to specify where good localities exist, for there is scarcely a stream in the State which is not bordered by forests of excellent timber.

All of these streams save the Missouri furnish water-power and good mill sites, and even the large springs of the Niangua afford the best water-power observed in the State. But steam has usually proved the most economical power for the manufacture of lumber, as the site can be selected with greater advantage.

FROM MR. HAWN'S REPORT—GEOLOGICAL SURVEY OF THE STATE.

Mr. HAWN's examination embraced only the section containing the land of the Hannibal and St. Joseph Railroad Company.

In the valley of Grindstone, sec. 8, township 57, R. 31, is found a red, chocolate-colored silicious clay or shale, which, from its similarity, in many respects, to a material extensively used in Ohio and other States as a pigment, would doubtless furnish a cheap and abundant material for that purpose. When ground in oil, the color may be varied by adding a small quantity of white-lead, lamp-black, or other cheap paint, to suit the taste. This kind of paint is highly useful, not only for ornamental purposes, but also for rendering roofs fire-proof, by applying several heavy coats to the shingles.

So soon as the oil evaporates, the strong coating of silicious matter left on the surface will prevent a roof from taking fire from sparks, or even large coals.

SOIL.—The soil, in all parts of the district, is fertile in the highest degree, with slight modifications, requiring only a different mode of culture, and the products adapted to different localities, to produce equal results. Perhaps the preponderance may be in favor of the limestone district, west of Grand river, especially when we take into consideration that the products best adapted to that region are those that now yield the greatest profit on the labor expended; but, should circumstances change, that preponderance would be lost.

At some few localities in this district, the soil is thin and heavy, in consequence of a superabundance of clay; but where it is properly tilled, and the subsoil is in reach of the plow, so as to be brought up and mixed with the surface, it becomes friable, and produces well. Such a soil is remarkably well adapted to the cereal products, maturing those plants without the addition of artificial stimulants, so apt to produce a redundancy of straw at the expense of a proper development of grain.

The soil of Macon county is remarkably well adapted to the production of a superior article of Tobacco; also, the upper portions of Chariton, the higher portions of Linn, and the southeastern portions of Livingston, and also the upper portions not included in the limestone district. These regions will become as famous for the production of superior tobacco, as were the most favored portions of Virginia in her palmiest days.

There is yet another variety of soil deserving attention. The alluvial deposits of the valley, usually denominated "Bottoms" in the west. This soil is necessarily deep, and of unbounded fertility; well adapted to the growth of Indian corn and hemp, but not to wheat and small grains, in consequence of its excessive fatness, or superabundance of organic matter.

4

In the valley of Grand river, the bottoms vary from three to five miles in width, and are elevated from twenty to thirty feet above the -bed, and above ordinary highwater mark. In the valley of Grand Chariton, the bottom lands are about equal in extent to those on Grand river, but not elevated so high above the bed of the stream, and are consequently more frequently inundated.

Timber usually exists in the valleys and along watercourses, of the usual varieties found in this State, and the west generally. The most abundant and valuable varieties are the different kinds of white and black oaks, black and white walnut, and occasionally a grove of maples. The supply would be sufficient for domestic and agricultural purposes, if it were equally distributed; especially when we take into consideration the facilities the Hannibal and St. Joseph Railroad will afford in distributing the products of the forest, and the coal beds found along that line.

The Osage Orange, too, is under extensive experiment here, and thus far promises well; and should success finally attend the rearing of hedges for fencing purposes, a small amount of timber will suffice this district.

It will be seen, by inspection of the map, that this district is traversed by several rivers, with their branches diverging in every direction, and watering the country in an admirable manner. The largest of these is Grand river, running nearly south through the center of the district. Grand Chariton is next in size. The volume of water is, perhaps, less than half that of Grand river, and, in almost all respects, the same Salt river discharges less water than Grand Chariton, and differs from it by being composed of alternate pools and rapids. These streams will afford no other facilities to the business of the country than in creating waterpower, for which Salt river and its branches are well adapted.

Several of the minor streams, too, are well suited to that purpose, particularly Medicine and Shoal creeks.

At Utica, Livingston county, an establishment is now in course of construction on an extensive scale; and, all things considered, I should suppose that a sufficient amount of water-power can be obtained to supply the domestic wants for many years to come.

There is but little waste land in this district. This circumstance, with the exceeding fertility and durability of the soil, and its adaptation to the various products of this climate, its inexhaustible beds of coal, and its salubrious climate, renders this a favored district, and capable of sustaining a population as dense as any other portion of equal extent in the northern temperate zone.

HEMP.

LETTER FROM C. R. ROGERS, Esq., OF MARION COUNTY.

MARION COUNTY, Mo., January 20, 1858.

J. T. K. HAYWARD, ESQ.

Dear Sir :—I am in the receipt of yours of the 8th, in which you request a statement of my mode of cultivating hemp, the cost per acre, etc., which I will give you in brief.

Hemp requires the dryest and richest land we have to insure success. It is best to take new land, and not cultivate it in any thing else. It may be grown on the same land fifteen or twenty years with equal success, allowing for the variation in seasons.

The best mode of preparing the ground is to plow deep, as early in the spring as the ground will admit; then let it lie in that state until about the first of May; then cross-plow with one-horse plows; sow one and a quarter bushels seed per acre; harrow in, and then cross-harrow. If the ground is dry and cloddy, roll as a finishing touch.

Hemp should not be cut too green, as the lint would be light. The leaves should commence falling off, and the stalk become a little yellow.

We use the common hook in cutting, as we can save it in a better manner, and a hand can cut as much as he can break out.

Hemp should be spread out to water late in October or early in November, as generally late spreading is the best.

The average yield is about 800 pounds per acre; the average price per cwt., for the last ten years, about five dollars.

The cost per acre, on an average, for the last ten years, is about as follows:

One and one-fourth bushels seed	$1.25
Sowing, ...	50
Plowing and harrowing, ...	2.50
Cutting (two hands one day), ...	2.00
Shocking, spreading, and re-shocking, ...	2.00
Breaking 800 lbs., at $1 per cwt., ...	8.00
Cost per acre, ...	$16.25
Value 800 lbs. hemp, at $5 per cwt., . . .	40.00
Net profit on one acre, ...	$23.75

A good hand can break six acres. The breaking is usually done in January, February, and March, as the weather may suit. Each hand has 100 lbs. per day for his task, and is paid for what he breaks over that amount, at the rate of one dollar per 100 lbs.

A hand can break from 100 to 200 lbs. per day.

Yours respectfully,   C. R. ROGERS.

GENERAL CROPS.

LETTER FROM JOHN NICHOLS, Esq., PRESIDENT MARION COUNTY AGRICULTURAL SOCIETY.

MARION COUNTY, Mo., May 17, 1858.

To WILLIAM CARSON,

Secretary Land Department H. & St. Jo. R. R. Co.

Dear Sir:—You request me to give you an account of the gross receipts from the productions of my farm, for the year 1856, with the cost of producing the various articles, and the net profits.

In reply, I will state that I have not kept sufficient memoranda, but will approximate as nearly as possible.

Having given Mr. HAYWARD a detailed statement of my mode of cultivating hemp, I will only state that the receipts for my hemp crop, for the year mentioned, amounted to the sum of $2,000; receipts for pork, same year, $1,200; beef, $300; wheat, $1,200; sheep, $50; cows and calves, $150; making the gross receipts, for the articles above mentioned, $4,900. Receipts for potatoes, fruit, dairy productions, etc., no particular account was kept; nor have I a minute account of the expenses of the family; but I have sufficient to know that the last-mentioned articles more than paid family expenses, store bills, smith's bills, etc.

To produce the above, I cultivated two hundred and fifty acres of land, and employed the labor of six hands, making the product of each hand about $816, and the clear profit on each acre of land cultivated, $19.60.

Very respectfully yours, JOHN NICHOLS.

HEMP.

LETTER FROM JUDGE LEONARD, OF PLATTE COUNTY.

HEMPLAND, March 6, 1858.

J. T. K. HAYWARD, ESQ., *Land Agent, etc.*

Dear Sir:—Owing to my absence from home, yours of January 8th was received only last night.

In reply to your inquiries touching the culture of hemp, I would observe that upon our best uplands, and in the vicinity of the Missouri river, with the best culture, I estimate one-half a tun, or 1,120 lbs., an average crop per acre. Of course, it will sometimes rise above and sometimes fall below, owing to seasons.

I estimate the average price at $100 per tun, net; but the price fluctuates greatly. It is now quoted considerably below a hundred in St. Louis; but for each of the three years past, for some portions of the year, it has ranged, in St. Louis, from $130 to $150 per tun, if I mistake not.

I estimate the expense of cultivating an acre of hemp at about $25, as follows:

Seed, one and one-fourth bushels,	$1.25
Pitching crop,	3.00
Cutting,	3.00
Breaking off leaves and putting into shocks,	1.00
Spreading,	50
Taking up after watered,	50
Breaking, per cwt., $1.25,	12.50
Baling,	1.50
Hauling to place of shipment,	1.75
	$25.00

The last item depends so entirely on distance of hauling, as to be unreliable in my general estimate.

If the crop is light, the breaking would be less; but it is more labor to break a given number of pounds when the yield is light than when it is heavy.

My estimate, then, for an average yield of an acre of our best uplands, with the best culture, after paying for seed and labor, is $25. If the land is inferior, this sum will not be realized. If the land is good, but the cultivation or management inferior, this sum will not be realized.

Upon a plantation of not less than five to ten field hands, I estimate, upon the hypothesis before stated, of the best land and the best cultivation, that they will average five and a half tuns per hand, or $350 per hand per year. And over and above this, they will raise grain and stock sufficient for their own and the subsistence of an ordinary sized family.

Few crops preserve the ground so well as hemp. In hemp culture, the land is not much exposed to wash; and I believe hemp growers are disagreed as to whether successive crops upon the same ground tend to its impoverishment. Cases are to be found in which ten or twelve successive crops have been raised upon the same ground with undiminished yield. Hemp leaves land in fine condition for other crops.

I am not aware of any country superior to the Missouri river country for the hemp culture, either as to quality or to quantity per acre.

If our hemp does not rank in the markets of the world as the equal of Russia, or any other, I apprehend it will be found owing to defective culture, or defective handling.

Owing to the dryness of our climate, we are relieved from the labor of stacking in the fall, as in Kentucky, and usually we have more weather in winter suitable to break hemp than there.

Yours, etc.,   S. L. LEONARD.

HEMP.

LETTER FROM COL. PFOUTS, OF BUCHANAN COUNTY.

ROCK HOUSE PRAIRIE, BUCHANAN Co., Mo.,
 January 23, 1858.

MR. J. T. K. HAYWARD.

Dear Sir:—Yours of the 8th inst. is at hand; and in answer thereto, I will say we have as fine land in Northwest Missouri as is to be found anywhere. I have never seen so large a body of rich land anywhere. We have an abundance of the very best water; plenty of timber in most places; and good health. No country is better adapted to the growing of hemp; and land that will produce good hemp, will produce any thing that is adapted to this climate. Wheat, corn, oats, tobacco, grass, and all kinds of vegetables, grow well here.

I have been farming here for eighteen years, and will give you my experience as to the cost of raising hemp.

For the last few years, labor has been much higher than it was years before, and hemp has borne a better price until the present. It is down now.

COST OF RAISING HEMP PER ACRE.

One and one-fourth bushels of seed, ...	$1.25
Plowing ground, harrowing, etc., ...	2.50
Cutting hemp, ...	4.00
Rolling, taking up, etc., ...	1.50
Breaking, $1.25 per hundred, ...	12.50
	$20.75

Product of an acre, 1,000 lbs.: take off the gross 12 lbs. on the hundred, leaving hemp 890 lbs., at 5 cents, ... $44.50

The price for many years has averaged five dollars per hundred, thus making $23.75 per acre over cost. One hand can take care of ten acres with some help in breaking; and he can raise an ordinary crop of grain, as hemp does not materially conflict with other crops.

The country back from the Missouri river is not so well adapted to hemp as that on the river. We are experimenting on the Chinese hemp. If it is what it is now believed to be, all the prairie land in North Missouri will produce good hemp, and the yield much larger than the kind now raised.

Yours respectfully,   V. PFOUTS.

HEMP.

LETTER FROM HON. WILLARD P. HALL.

ST. JOSEPH, Mo., January 26, 1858.

J. T. K. HAYWARD, Esq., *Hannibal.*

My Dear Sir:—I am in receipt of your letter of the 8th inst., and in reply to your inquiries, I have to say that the quality of hemp grown here is first rate; the yield per acre is about eight hundred weight, and the price per hundred weight is about five dollars.

It is difficult for me to state the precise cost of making and preparing a hemp crop for market, because our hemp growers generally own the hands they employ. It is usually considered that one good hand can grow and prepare for market ten acres of hemp. This, at the yield and price above stated, gives four hundred dollars as the earning of each good hand engaged in producing hemp, from that crop alone; and, as the hemp crop interferes but little with the corn and fall wheat crops, and partially only with several other crops, a prudent hemp farmer may calculate very certainly upon clearing at least four hundred dollars a year to each hand employed in cultivating hemp; his other crops paying all expenses.

The following statement of the cost of making and preparing a hemp crop for market, it is believed, will be found correct:

Breaking up ground, per acre, ... $2.00
Harrowing ground before sowing, ...50
One and a half bushels of seed, ... 1.50
Growing seed, ...25
Harrowing and cross-harrowing after sowing, per acre, 1.00
Cutting hemp, ... 3.00
Taking up hemp after cutting, ... 1.00
Spreading hemp to rot, ... 1.00
Taking up hemp after rotting, ... 1.00
Breaking up hemp, at one cent per pound, . . . 8.96

$20.21

Price of crop at 8 cwt. per acre, $5 per cwt., . . 40.00

Profit per acre, ... $19.79

Very respectfully your obedient servant,

WILLARD P: HALL.

HEMP.

LETTER FROM HON. ROB. WILSON, OF ANDREW COUNTY.

ANDREW COUNTY, Mo., February 13, 1858.

Hemp is extensively cultivated in the counties of Platte,
Buchanan, and Andrew. The soil in the counties of Holt,
Atchison, Nodaway, Clinton, Caldwell, Davies, and Livingston,
are believed to be well adapted to the growth of hemp, and
upon the completion of the Hannibal and St. Joseph Railroad,
several of the counties last-named will doubtless engage largely
in producing it.

The cost of raising an acre of hemp may be summed up as
follows:

For breaking land and sowing seed, ... $2.25
One and a half bushels seed, at $1.50, ... 2.25
Cutting, ... 1.75
Shocking, ...75
Spreading, ... 1.25
Taking up and reshocking, ... 1.25
Breaking 1000 lbs., average crop, ... 10.09
Board of hands 16 days, ... 4.00

CREDIT. $23.50

By 1000 lbs. hemp, at $5 per cwt., ... 50.00

Being a balance in favor of producer, . $26.50

5

From this must be deducted for rent of land, and moving the article to market. Land in order for hemp, usually rents at about $3 per acre.

St. Joseph is the market for this section of country, and the cost of delivering hemp there is dependent on distance, roads, etc. Farmers usually deliver their hemp without much actual cost, with their own teams, and at such times as best suits their convenience.

One thousand pounds is considered, in this section of the State, a good average crop; but, in many instances, as high as 1,600 has been reached.

One hand can manage ten acres of hemp, do all the labor from first to last, and also raise sufficient of other crops to support himself and family; thus having, at the end of the year, a clear profit of $235 above the value of his labor, on the article of hemp alone.

I have been engaged in the cultivation of hemp for many years, and find it one of our most certain crops. The failures are few and far between.

The production of hemp does not injure the soil. Fields that have been cropped for many years, continue to yield as fair returns as new land.

The quality of hemp raised in this section of the State is believed to be fully equal to any raised in any part of the United States; and, when properly handled, sells for the highest price in all the principal markets.

A very large portion of the land in Northwest Missouri is well adapted to the growth of hemp, and much of it is not yet in cultivation, waiting for an accession of population.

Respectfully,   R. WILSON.

VIEW OF IMPROVED LANDS IN LIVINGSTON COUNTY.

TOBACCO.

LETTER FROM J. H. GENTRY, Esq., OF RALLS COUNTY.

FAIRMOUNT, RALLS Co., January 25, 1858.

MR. HAYWARD,

Dear Sir :—I received your letter requesting me to give you some information in relation to the culture of tobacco, and I embrace this opportunity of addressing you a few lines upon the subject. The first thing you wish to know is the actual cost of raising an acre of tobacco, and making it ready for market. Well, sir, my cultivation in tobacco has been so much mixed up with other crops, and the labor done by hands consisting of men and boys, that it would be almost impossible to estimate the cost of raising the crop; but it is estimated that a good hand will manage from three to four acres of tobacco, and cultivate an ordinary crop of corn, wheat, and oats.

The best mode of raising tobacco, according to my experience, is to take fresh timbered land, break it up well, harrow it well, and, after taking off the roots, check it off three and a half feet each way, and set the plants in the middle of the square, or edge of the furrow.

The quality of tobacco, in this country, varies with the quality of the land. Rich land will produce heavy, coarse tobacco, and nearly double the quantity of thin land; but the difference in quality, if well managed, will about make up for the difference in quantity; for you may know that fine tobacco is worth double as much as coarse. I have made from $30 to $100 per acre from tobacco, but $40 per acre I consider a fair average; that is 800 lbs. per acre, at an average price of $5 per cwt.

Having given you such facts in relation to tobacco raising (in my brief way) as I am in possession of, I now subscribe myself,

Your obedient servant,   J. H. GENTRY.

To J. T. K. HAYWARD, *Land Agent H. & St. Jo. R. R.*

TOBACCO.

LETTER FROM JUDGE G. WILLIAMSON, OF MONROE CO.

MONROE COUNTY, January 16, 1858.

J. T. K. HAYWARD, ESQ.

Dear Sir:—Having received a communication from you, requesting information in regard to the culture of tobacco, I, at the earliest convenient opportunity, will give you my views in regard to your inquiry in regard to the said crop.

In the first place, you wished to know what it would cost to raise a crop, and prepare it for market. One good hand can cultivate and save two and a half acres in ordinary seasons, besides attending other crops. If his whole attention was turned to raising tobacco, he could cultivate some five acres, if the worms should not be too numerous, which is sometimes the case. But there have been fewer worms in Missouri than there have been in Kentucky or Virginia.

As to preparing it for market, in this country, there is very little preparation necessary, as we generally sell in the hand, tied up in two classes, good and lugs, and tied up in as large hands as you can well hold in your hand; and our stripping and tieing up we generally do in bad weather, when we could do nothing else well; and we generally sell in Hannibal.

The cost of hauling to market is from 40 to 50 cents per cwt. If we should press in hogsheads, we have to tie it up in small hands, say about six leaves in a hand, and to be very neat and very particular in regard to the order that it is in.

The cost of pressing and furnishing hogsheads is about two dollars per cwt. We generally prefer to sell it in the hand, as we can get it to market much earlier.

As to yield per acre, it depends upon the season. In ordinary seasons, the yield is from eight to twelve hundred pounds per acre; and upon good manured land, there may be 1,400 lbs. to the acre; but that is rather an extra crop.

As to the price, it varies much. The crop for 1856 was sold, in this neighborhood, for eight and ten dollars per hundred, tied up in large hands, in Hannibal. For the year

1857, our crops sold, in this neighborhood, from $6 to $6.50 per cwt., in the hand, tied up in the same way.

There are a few that have not sold at these prices. They prefer pressing to selling at these prices; but, for my part, I should always prefer selling in the hand at the prices named.

As to the quality of the crop, there is, in my opinion, no country better adapted to the culture of tobacco, nor would the quality be surpassed anywhere, if there was sufficient inducements offered for the management of the article; but the buyers generally give the same price, in the same neighborhood, whether the article is good or not. If the buyers would buy according to quality, and pay an equivalent, there would be, then, some inducements for us to take pains in raising a good article, and then, I repeat it, this section of the county could not be beat anywhere, especially in the timbered lands.

The prairies are not so good for tobacco as the timbered land, as it is longer maturing, though we raise some very good tobacco on prairie land, especially when it is manured; but not so pretty an article generally. It is rather dark, or brown, but very heavy.

I have now answered your inquiries to the best of my judgment, and I have had a good deal of experience in the article.

I remain yours with respect,

GEORGE WILLIAMSON.

TOBACCO.

LETTER FROM J. D. SMITH, Esq., OF MACON COUNTY.

At Home, February 13, 1858.

J. T. K. HAYWARD, *Hannibal, Mo.*

Dear Sir:—I have received your letter, making inquiries in relation to the culture of tobacco in this county.

From some experience in the businesss, I am prepared to make the following statements:

First.—The cost of raising and preparing an acre of tobacco for market is between twenty and thirty dollars.

Second.—The average yield per acre is about one thousand pounds.

Third.—The price at which sales are made, depends on the demand and quality of the article—usually ranging from four to ten dollars per hundred.

Fourth.—The quality of the article depends on the quality of the soil in which it is grown. Prairie land produces a coarse, heavy article, which usually comes of a dark color. Timbered land produces a finer article. This quality commands a better price in market than that which is grown on prairie land. Our best quality of soil, (which is white oak timbered,) produces tobacco which is unsurpassed in quality by any other section of the State.

Tobacco raising is considered a profitable business by those engaged in it.

Hands can be employed in its cultivation, which are not able to perform heavy manual labor. One able hand can cultivate and manage about five acres.

There is as much tobacco raised in this county as any other in the State; and would be much more if the farmers could find a ready market at home.*

Yours respectfully,   J. D. SMITH.

TOBACCO.

LETTER FROM COL. M. M. TOWNER, OF MACON COUNTY.

BLOOMINGTON, MACON Co., Mo., }
January 23, 1858.   }

COL. WM. CARSON,

Sir:—In answer to your letter relative to my experience in the culture and management of tobacco, and the adaptation of the soil of this county to the growth of the article, I beg leave to state that I have produced the WEED, and have been engaged in stemming, pressing, and shipping the article, and from my experience, I am satisfied the soil of Macon county

---

* This will be afforded by opening the road.

is well adapted to its growth. A very fine article of manufacturing is produced; and, with proper management, an article equal to the best VIRGINIA can be produced here. The average yield per acre is about 1000 pounds, though as much as 2,100 pounds has been produced to the acre, and the article can be produced for $3 per 100 lbs. The average price obtained by our farmers for the last five years is about $5 per 100 lbs.

The value of this crop compares favorably with other crops. To men of small means, it pays better than any other crop. To men of large means, stock raising pays, perhaps, better with us.

Our farmers have not as yet cultivated tobacco extensively, but have produced from $30,000 to $75,000 worth per year.

With railroad facilities for transporting their crops to market, its growth will be greatly increased, and will yield to the producer a greater profit.

Tobacco growers, in my opinion, can find no country more favorable to a profitable production of this article than in Macon county.

Respectfully,   M. M. TOWNER.

WHEAT.

LETTER FROM JAMES GLASSCOCK, ESQ., OF RALLS COUNTY.

SAVERTON TOWNSHIP, RALLS CO., MO., }
May 24, 1858.   }

To WILLIAM CARSON,

    Secretary Land Department H. & St. Jo. R. R.

Dear Sir:—In answer to yours, I state that my father settled in the wood in 1823, on what was considered poor land, and gave his attention to the culture of wheat and other grains. I might say, he introduced the successful culture of wheat into this part of Missouri; for up to that time it was said that nearly all the wheat turned to cheat.

His first crop, in 1823, of sixteen acres, yielded thirty bushels per acre, supposed, as the ground was not measured.

The wonder was that there was so little cheat among .t. All this crop was sold for seed, at fifty cents per bushel.

He continued to cultivate one-third of the cleared land in wheat every year, making from 500 to 1000 bushels a year, never making a failure—average price about fifty cents per bushel—to the year 1836, when I succeeded him on the same farm, where I have continued to the present time, never having made but one failure, in 1857. Then I raised about twenty bushels of spring wheat to the acre, on about thirty acres—the fall wheat being winter killed.

We did not take the pains to measure our ground or grain until the first Ralls County Fair, held in 1854. That year I got the premium for the largest yield of wheat, without extra preparation, which was a little less than thirty bushels to the acre, on five acres. My crop of 1,200 bushels sold at $2 per bushel.

In 1855, Mr. McCormick got the premium on the yield of fifty-eight bushels and sixteen pounds to the acre. Public opinion was, that there must have been some mistake in measurement; but, on hearing the testimony, I am convinced that it is within a fraction of being correct. That year I got the premium on oats, at seventy-four bushels to the acre. The next year my neighbor, Judge Stout, obtained the premium on wheat—yield, forty-one bushels to the acre. My crop that year was a good one, about 2000 bushels, which averaged me about $1.25 per bushel.

I have not kept an accurate account of my sales and expenditures to give the net income, but we make more than enough to live on without the wheat. I would remark that the timbered lands, between the high prairies and the bottoms on the rivers, are the best for wheat.

As to my mode of cultivation, I have not followed a uniform system, because I have been clearing land and adding new fields every year; but I prefer fallow lands, broken early in the summer, and kept bare of vegetation until September, when it should be sown or drilled. There is one of my neighbors, Enoch Symms, who has cultivated one piece of ground in wheat every year for the last eighteen years, without any decrease, and never missed a crop but one year, when it was winter killed.

I would remark, that when my father settled here, there was but one family living within five miles of us, and perhaps not one hundred bushels of wheat raised; and I believe, if the season continues favorable, there will be 20,000 bushels made within five miles of my house this year.

I would remark, that the State abounds in such a variety of soil, that there is no crop but there is land to suit it. The high bluffs for grapes and peaches; the hills for wheat and other small grain; the richest lands for hemp, corn and potatoes; and the watered lands for meadow and grass.

Yours, etc.,   JAMES GLASSCOCK.

GENERAL CROPS.

LETTER FROM JAMES G. LONGMIRE, Esq., OF MARION CO.

MARION COUNTY, Mo., May 17, 1858.

To WILLIAM CARSON,

Secretary Land Department H. & St. Jo. R. R.

Dear Sir:—I have received your note requesting me to give you an account of the productions of my farm, cost of producing, the gross amount, sales and net profits, and such other remarks as I might think proper to make.

In reply, I have to say that from my farm-book, I can give you a correct account of sales from my farm, for any given year, since 1848, and they vary according to various circumstances, such as the fruitfulness of the seasons, state of the market, etc. For instance; for the year 1848, my sales were for wheat $496; for hemp $2,384; for pork $757; sundries $67; making a gross amount $3,704.

I will here also state, that on the first day of January, 1848, I took an invoice of all my property, land, and stock employed, and found the aggregate value of which was $9,350.

My whole expense for labor, ordinary family expenses included, was $1,920, leaving a clear profit of $1,784, being about 19 per cent. on the capital; but it must be noted that I made improvements on my farm worth $500 or $600. My sales for 1850 were total $2,843; expenses, as above, $1,300; clear profits, $1,543.

To produce the above, I have employed, on an average, the labor of six hands, at a cost of $150 each. Since 1850, I have devoted my attention to feeding stock, principally cattle and hogs, in addition to the ordinary crops of wheat, corn, hemp, oats, etc.; and I find, owing to the admirable adaptation of our soil to the different grasses—blue grass, timothy, and clover—that stock raising can be made the most profitable branch of our agricultural operations. In fact, I have no hesitancy in saying, that from a careful and close observation for ten years, I am fully convinced that Missouri is destined to be the greatest grazing State in the Union.

I will further state, that some of the lands of Northeast Missouri have been very much underrated in former years, for want of knowledge of the chemical properties of the soils, and consequently not knowing the kind of crop each variety of soil is best adapted to produce. But since the geological survey of the State by Prof. SWALLOW, we have ascertained that much of our poorest looking lands have inexhaustible stores of fertility lying under the surface, in the form of marl; the subsoil being, in many places, superior to the surface soil.—(Geological Survey of Missouri, p. 184.)

I have cut two tuns of timothy hay per acre, on sixty acres of land, on an average, for six years.

I could give you a more minute account of products and sales for different years, but I hope the foregoing will suffice.

Yours very respectfully,

JAMES G. LONGMIRE.

GENERAL CROPS.

LETTER FROM MAJOR W. L. IRVINE, OF DE KALB CO.

DE KALB COUNTY, Mo., January 22, 1858.

Dear Sir:—Your favor of the 9th has just been received, requesting me to give you a statement of the agricultural resources, healthfulness, etc., of this 'portion of the country, and I hasten to answer in the order presented.

Timber, in this section of the country, good; as yet but little coal discovered; average depth of wells on upland thirty feet; stock water abundant; supply of stone good; clay answers well for making bricks. The soil and climate are well adapted to the culture of hemp; the average yield per acre 1000 lbs.; some crops under favorable culture have reached 1,700 to the acre; cost of raising and preparing the crop for market, $16 per acre; average price, the past five years, has been $90 per tun, ready for shipment. Hemp is regarded as the most profitable crop.

The quantity of tobacco raised per acre is good; the quality not the best.

The country is well adapted to the raising of corn and wheat, especially wheat. The yield in all the small grain crops is large. Horses, mules, cattle, and sheep do well. The country is decidedly healthy, and is rapidly improving, and when our internal improvements are completed, will make it a great country.

Respectfully,   WILLIAM L. IRVINE.

GENERAL CROPS.

LETTER FROM C. R. ROGERS, Esq., OF MARION COUNTY.

MARION COUNTY, Mo., May 17, 1858.

To WILLIAM CARSON,
  Secretary Land Department H. & St. Jo. R. R. Co.

Dear Sir:—In reply to your request that I should inform you as to the gross receipts from my farm for the year 1856, from all the productions thereof, the cost of producing the various articles, and the net profits, I have to state that I have not kept sufficient memoranda to give minutely all the information you desire; but, from the data I have, I will give you the statement, disregarding fractions.

Having given to Mr. HAYWARD a particular account of the culture of hemp, I need not refer to that here, further than to say that the receipts for my hemp crop, for the year mentioned, amounted to the sum of $3,200; receipts for pork, $1000; beef, $1000; wheat, $600; mules, $2000; making the gross receipts for the articles mentioned, $7,800. From this is to be deducted, for extra labor in cutting and breaking hemp, $400; cash outlay for mule colts, $1000; for stock hogs, $250; for cattle, $130; cash outlay for family expenses, $500; amounting to $2,280; which, deducted from $7,800, leaves the net balance $5,520. I say net balance, because the receipts for fruit crops, potatoes, dairy, etc., were sufficient to pay merchants' and smiths' bills, and all the ordinary expenses of the family, except as above stated.

I have plow-land in cultivation on my farm 310 acres, and to cultivate it, employ labor equal to six hands. Raising and feeding mules is quite a profitable business here. Formerly colts, at weaning, could be bought at from $15 to $30; but recently have gone up to from $40 to $60, and even as high as $75; but the price of grown mules has advanced in proportion, and the profits on feeding mules from one to two years ranges from 40 to 100 per cent. Oats is a very certain and productive crop here, and our highland prairies are admirably adapted to the growth of timothy and other grasses.

C. R. ROGERS.

www.ingramcontent.com/pod-product-compliance
Lightning Source LLC
Chambersburg PA
CBHW022152020726
47496CB00008B/2677